The Final Stand

The Final Stand

Sreeraj Mannattil

Published in India by Zorba Books, 2016

Website: www.zorbabooks.com
Email: info@zorbabooks.com

ISBN Print Book – 978-93-85020-78-0
ISBN eBook – 978-93-85020-79-7

Zorba Books Pvt. Ltd.(opc)

Gurgaon, INDIA

Printed at : Repro Knowledgecast Limited, Thane

Dedication

To a cute little girl, my family and a couple
of weird creatures with whom I can discuss anything
ranging from rocket science to dirty jokes.

Acknowledgement

To the mighty lord Shiva and Shani

Content

The beginning

The origin of the world started with an *omkara* that released the energy from a zero-sized particle and caused expansion in all possible directions.

The universe had to start from some point…otherwise none of us would be here.

But don't worry if you don't believe this. Believe in your own theories as the entire world is running on theories either propagated or followed. Life is much beyond our perception and each of us has a reason to be here. Everything that we see has a beginning and an end. The aim of life is to understand the sole reason of our existence. But there is no need to worry if you fail in this mission.

Because there is something powerful called karma that is a good leveller for your deeds. Some people call it fate, but this fate was already chosen by your karma.

There are rebirths, suffering and joy in your life because it is your karma that has brought it into your life. Never get carried away or lose yourself in victories and failures because your life is a script that has already been written.

I don't mind being called mad or insane because in madness lies the true beauty of life.

The sons of gods are still alive in this world to protect it from evil.

The story starts here…

Chapter 1
14th September, 2008
NH-47

Shankaran's forehead was covered in sweat as he emerged from a prominent hotel in Chennai. He had just had a meeting with some people he had never hoped to see in his life. As one of the assistants of Travancore Palace, Shankaran felt a pang of guilt at having disclosed the secret that his family had protected for hundreds of years.

His hand firmed its grip on the suitcase that would change his fortune forever. It contained about twenty million Indian rupees in cash and jewels as had been promised. He had initially rejected the offer, but the mounting pressure on him and his family in the form of life-threatening calls led him to divulge the details of the treasures inside the hidden vaults of the temple.

The meeting was arranged by a prominent public figure in India. He was brought to Chennai from Trivandrum by car to avoid any suspicion. He had taken leave on the pretext of visiting his son studying engineering in a private college in Chennai. The meeting was attended by two foreigners and the politician, who also doubled up as the interpreter. Shankaran did not know the nationality of the foreigners.

He entered the room and was offered a drink even before the meeting started. Having never seen that brand of liquor before, its smoothness compelled him to ask for another glass. He felt relaxed after that drink, and definitely much bolder.

"Welcome Mr. Shankaran," one of the foreigners pronounced his name with a little difficulty.

Although much emboldened by the drinks, Shankaran seemed to choke on his words. He started mumbling, and was eventually saved by the politician who interfered at just the right time. "Shankaran is tired after his long journey," he said.

"Take it easy," said one of the foreigners. Then, continuing in a serious tone, "Is he willing to provide us with all the information we need?"

"Yes he is! Provided we satisfy him with what he has asked for."

They promptly handed over the suitcase to him. Shankaran told them about the wealth inside the temple, while passing on a map of the layout of the vault neatly sketched on a piece of cloth. The map had been in their family for a long time, and his father who had given it to him had made him promise not to ever disclose its existence.

Shankaran got into the car to go back to Trivandrum soon after. Although he was tired, he was scared of falling off to sleep. He clutched his suitcase tightly as he sat at the edge of the seat. He called his wife to inform her that he was on his way back and would reach the next afternoon. His father's feeble body lying on the bed swam before his eyes with his words echoing in his mind, "Never break a promise made to the king." At the same time, an image of the god Padmanabha also flashed in front of his eyes.

Just as he was about to close his eyes for his much-needed nap, a trailer from the opposite side rammed into their vehicle, dragging them about 30 feet along the highway that was lined by dry rocky hills.

The next day, all the newspapers' front pages were filled with the story of the tragic end of a loyal servant of the Travancore king. As per the reports, he was travelling back to his hometown in a car belonging to a friend he had met in Chennai, with just a suitcase containing some clothes and a cell phone. Nobody suspected any foul play in the death of an erstwhile loyal employee of a diminishing kingdom.

Chapter 2
5th October, 2008
Shri Padmanabha Temple Trivandrum

Just about a year ago, a mammoth treasure was discovered inside the vaults of the temple. What was presumed to be some information from a devotee actually opened the door to a treasure chest that nobody had ever imagined existed.

It was a usual day at the temple. Like always, there was a huge rush of Padmanabha devotees trying to get a view of the idol. The priests started chanting and there was an air of calmness all around.

Suddenly, the sound of the chants was broken by the sound of choppers that seemed to have appeared out of nowhere. Before the choppers even landed, dozens of heavily armed people with sophisticated weapons jumped out of them. They seemed to know exactly what they had to do. The security forces deployed at the temple were no match for the kind of assault they unleashed.

Within seconds, all the guards were ruthlessly murdered. The mercenaries walked into treasure vault confidently. It was as if they had been there before or were trained very thoroughly. They used a high-intensity grenade to blow up the door and two of them entered the vault through the smoke and debris.

The duo entering the vault had a map with them. They stopped for a few seconds to study it, looked around, nodded at each other and walked in confidently. The map contained the location of an object they were after. They found the intricately carved wooden box with the Hindu symbol Om carved on it. Since they had clear instructions to not open the box, they quickly picked it up and started to leave, when they suddenly noticed the other treasures inside the vault. Their mouths opened in disbelief. But since they were instructed to not touch anything else inside the vault, they quickly turned and walked back out. With their mission accomplished, they all got into the chopper patting each other's backs and smiling knowing that they were on their way to becoming billionaires.

The chopper carried them to a remote island in the sea, where a small plane had been waiting for their return. The leader of the group opened a bottle of champagne to celebrate the success of their mission.

Two fighter jets accompanied the small plane carrying the mercenaries to a secret lab in the Alpine valley.

Chapter 3

5th September, 2008
The Minister's Flight

Karthik Devarajan was on his way back to Delhi from Bangalore after the conference on green energy. The minister of power was on a chartered flight finishing up some work related to the supply of nuclear power technology from Russia to boost energy production in India.

The flight took off from the airport just as the minister started going through the contract papers. As one of the better educated ministers in the government, he was known to have vast knowledge of the economics of energy. He was accompanied by his secretary, one of the senior-most bureaucrats of the country, and his security guards.

Karthik Devarajan came from a middle-class family and had found his way up to the ministry by the dint of his hard work and experience in handling the various power projects executed within India. He had been invited into politics by a prominent political party and soon became an active member of the political institution in India.

The government had decided to set up a nuclear power plant in Arankulam and had floated global tenders for the supply of technology for it. Devarajan was able to negotiate a good deal with Russia at the most competent rates through his experience and expertise in the field. Although there was a lot of pressure on him from multinational giants in the field of technology supply, he was not the type to succumb to pressure tactics.

Suddenly, there was a huge jerk and everyone inside the aircraft started panicking. As the intensity of the jerks and turbulence increased, people scrambled around the aircraft with someone chanting aloud. The engine started bellowing smoke and making a sound that indicated engine failure. The pilot seemed to have lost control and was trying to reach the airbase through frantic signals. The plane started free falling midway through the air and burnt to cinders within minutes of crash landing in an isolated forest area in Maharashtra.

During investigations later, it was determined that the charter had been arranged much before the journey. The plane belonged to the fleet reserved for ministers and was one of the best maintained aircraft among the fleet.

Further investigations revealed that just before the flight took off, two men with authorized ID cards entered the aircraft on the pretext of some last-minute checks and did some work on the engine. None of the officials suspected anything because it was not unusual to do checks before a flight.

The next morning, the world was agog with the news of the accidental death of a cabinet minister. All the television channels kept showing high-profile people from various fields expressing their condolences and views about the death.

Miles away from the airport from where the flight took off, two charred bodies were found in a state beyond recognition. It was determined that they were the same people who had done the last minute maintenance of the aircraft before the flight.

Soon, the case was taken over by the National Investigation Agency to quell the various rumours about the accident.

Chapter 4

30th August 2008
Lothskid Secret Chambers, London

Lothskid is one of the oldest banks of the world. It controlled the economy of the whole world and was naturally connected to the heads of leading economies, political parties and religious heads. Headquartered in London, it was known for funding media activities all around the world to maintain economic conditions.

A secret meeting was planned at the Lothskid chambers to discuss the two important issues that had been bothering the officials. Apart from them, there were representatives from some other nation's secret agencies at the meeting. One was an American, another belonged to Southeast Asia, and the last person in the group was of British origin. The first thing on the agenda was the setback faced in the energy deal with India. The second was about the secret discovery of a Lothskid official through a satellite.

The meeting started immediately without any formalities. The lights were dimmed as some satellite images projected on a screen on the wall showed an object like a small eggshell. As the representatives wondered what it was they were looking at, a voice spoke from the corner of the room breaking the silence. The owner of the voice was a neatly dressed man wearing round-rimmed spectacles. All attention turned to him as he detailed the object enthusiastically.

He belonged to the scientific department of Lothskid that explored the world with its satellite which had high-definition scanners. He said, "During one of my explorations of the southern part of India, I located a particular object in an ancient temple. What aroused my curiosity was its structure and properties. It emitted a certain energy in the form of controlled waves that had a higher frequency than all known rays on Earth, but it seemed to be neutralized by the box in which it was kept. However, the density of the object was infinite because it was difficult to percolate by any frequency of waves."

The chairperson asked, "How is the object of any help to us? What applications does it have?"

Buoyed by the question, the scientist responded, "If the object is fully explored and properly identified, it will change the course of future weapon technology. This tiny object has the power to cause unimaginable destruction. It is an alternative to the presently available nuclear bombs."

"How could they invent something like that?" asked the chairperson in awe.

"The technology of ancient India is beyond our understanding. We have yet to learn about what they used for weapons in that parts of the world," the scientist replied humbly.

"The second thing is that a nuclear reactor is being set up in India with technological help from Russia. The bad part is that they have refused our offer for the project technology, and hence the dependability of our company in the future too. And it is your duty to stop the project. Somehow we must build some negative stories about the technology provided by Russia," said the chairperson feverishly to the American.

"I agree. For this, we will need to involve someone local and use the media effectively to spread the propaganda," answered the American. "The good thing is that we have found already identified someone who can help us," he continued.

"To start with, we need to eliminate the present minister of power of India, Karthik Devarajan. He has been the biggest hurdle for us," said the chairman.

The first resolution was to get hold of the secret object by any means. The object was to be brought to Lothskid's secret lab for experiments. The second resolution had a larger political significance. It was to obstruct the construction of a nuclear reactor plant in India. "If the nuclear facility is constructed, India will not have any energy crisis in the future and its dependability on the multinational company that offered them various energy solutions will end. Also, the offer of the supply of technology to this particular nuclear plant through the US-based arm of the company had been rejected. Instead, a cheaper indigenous method was used. The success of the self-developed technology was definitely a potential threat to the company's business interests in the nuclear energy field.

The third and final resolution was the assassination of the minister of power of India, for which arrangements had already been made.

Chapter 5

6th October, 2008
NIA Headquarters, Delhi

Vinod Raju, head of NIA, was deeply occupied in his thoughts since the morning as he tried to connect the three notorious incidents that had taken place in the last couple of weeks – the accidental death of the cabinet minister; the burglary of a secret object from a famous temple; and the death of a royal servant to the kingdom of Travancore.

The most confusing thing was that nothing other than the secret object was taken from the temple even though it had a huge amount of gold and money in it. He just couldn't make sense of it. What was the motive for the burglary? Especially considering the nature and the persons involved. What was the object?

He was awaiting a call from his assistant Prabudh Bhattacharya who was at the temple and had started his investigations already. Since nothing else was missing from the temple, could the object have a religious significance? If so, what could it be? And who was behind it? His mind kept going around in circles.

Suddenly, something struck him and he quickly made a phone call to the ISRO office.

"ISRO, how can I help you?" the voice on the other side answered. It was Vaidhyanathan, widely regarded as a genius in the field of space research in India.

"Hi Vaidhya, it's me Vinod. How have you been? Have you heard about the recent developments?" .

"Hello Vinod, good to hear from you. Yes, I heard about the incidents – really unfortunate. How can I be of any help?"

"I need some information about any unusual flight movements on the same day near the Kerala seashore," said Vinod

Considering gravity of the situation, Vaidhyanadhan readily agreed to cooperate with the NIA chief. He immediately made a call to the RISAT team, the satellite that monitored the borders for infiltrations, to get the satellite images of flying objects around the Arabian Sea coast on 5th October 2008.

The recorded satellite images showed a mysterious flight traced to the borders of Pakistan, and the details were conveyed to the NIA. It confirmed the chief's worst nightmare – that there was a foreign agency engaged in a secret mission on Indian soil. However, there was still no answer that the object that was stolen and the motive for stealing it. It was imperative that he find out what the object was for more clarity on the issue.

Although the cause of Shankaran's death became somewhat clearer, it was still shrouded in mystery. He had some vital clues about the meeting held in Chennai in the presence of a prominent person, and also the large transaction of money from a foreign source to an NGO's account. The involvement of the same person in some other dealings was further confirmed by his counterpart in another secret Indian agency.

His assistant, Prabudh Upadhyay called to inform him about a yogi he had met during his investigations. The person had, during the course of conversation, expressed his desire to meet the chief of investigations to explain something related to the theft. Apparently, he was at the temple when the daring theft took place. The NIA chief agreed to meet the yogi at the predesignated isolated place.

The unknown yogi's calm aura made the chief feel completely at ease. With a soft voice, he welcomed them, "Very nice to meet you sir."

"Good to meet you too. What do you want to tell me?" he came straight to the point.

Raju couldn't believe what he was hearing. "The shell," explained the yogi, "contains the most powerful weapon in the universe and is made of unidentified materials."

Apparently, it was based on the origin of the universe, the start of the big bang that resonates with the sound of ohm. He continued, "The densely packed sub-atomic particles have an infinite density, and move around randomly inside the shell made with an impenetrable material." He explained that it had been passed down various privileged Hindu dynasties before being kept inside the vault to protect it.

"How do you know so much about it?" the chief inquired a little skeptically.

"I belong to a society that you have never heard about. You will know when the time comes," replied the yogi with a mysterious smile.

Chapter 6
6th November, 2008
The Uprising of Arankulam

The engineers and labourers were hard at work when the drama outside the proposed nuclear power plant started. Hundreds of people had gathered to protest the construction of the nuclear plant. Panicked, the project manager had called the local police station asking for security. The huge crowd included a cross-section of society – there were religious leaders, politicians, people from various NGOs, and ordinary men, women and children. They all lived in the area and usually met in the evening at the shops and on the roads, but none of them had ever shown any kind of resistance in the past.

Their placards carried messages and cautions against nuclear power with some even displaying the hazards of a potential failure of the plant. Getting wind of the whole *tamasha,* the media had already gathered and set up their cameras to get the latest to their viewers. It seemed like there was a lot of money spent in arranging and coordinating the protest.

As the crowd increased, the people started to break through the security barriers becoming rowdier. The nuclear plant guards started getting flustered and this gave way to more chaos. The workers of the plant began to assemble together fearing attack from the villagers. Luckily, the police arrived to diffuse the situation. However, when some locals started attacking the police, the situation became even more volatile. Work came to a halt as the workers were quickly evacuated to safer places.

About a week prior to this incident, there had been a meeting between the local leaders and members of a few NGOs at a beachside hotel in Trivandrum. The prominent political person who was present Shankaran's meeting with the foreigners was also there. The meeting continued for about three hours.

"All you have to do is stop the construction of this plant," said the political figure to the local leaders.

"But on what ground? Which government agencies are involved in this project?" they asked.

"On safety grounds. And these people will help you with the details you need," he replied, gesturing towards a few people who were part of a leading NGO. The well-dressed lady and the two men waved back enthusiastically.

While leaving, each of the local leaders was seen carrying suitcases. Within a few hours, they reached their designated place where they were meeting the prominent people of the villages. The money was quickly distributed to them and the date of next the protest was fixed. It seemed much easier to convince the locals who had little education about the potential hazards of the nuclear power plants.

Money was not a constraint for the protest and everything was planned and coordinated by the NGOs. There was food for the protesters and a local centre had assured the participating villagers a certain amount as a daily wage. The protest resulted in a temporary halt of the construction of the nuclear plant.

Meanwhile the political leader enjoyed his daily drink with some important personalities of the area to enjoy the success of his plan. The ultimate reward for his service would be a seat in the central cabinet within a few days. Two days later, the media covered the emergence of a local politician who was suddenly initiated into a cabinet rank with the promise of closing the gap created by the shortage of energy in the nation.

Chapter 7

The Concept of Divine
Hands 3ʳᵈ BC – the Present

The last king known to have had the ownership of the sacred shell was King Ashoka, emperor of the Mauryas. He had inherited it from his father, Bindusara, who had received it from Chandragupta Maurya. Dejected with the brutalities of the Kalinga War, King Ashoka abdicated his throne and kingdom to lead a simple life.

However, he knew that he had to protect the divine shell passed down to him through the generations somehow, because he knew what impact it could have on the world. Bimbisara had narrated the story of the sacred shell to his son just before he died, and apprised him of the huge responsibility of protecting it. He advised to him to pass it on to safe hands after him.

In keeping with his father's words, after converting to Buddhism, Ashoka decided to hand it over to someone outside his kingdom because he found his heirs incapable of protecting the shell. He gave it to Uthiyan Cheralathan, king of a lesser-known kingdom, but also one of his closest allies.

The Chera kingdom shared its boundaries with the Mauryan kingdom, and as the king of the Cheras, Uthiyan

Cheralathan enjoyed special privileges in the courts of Ashoka. He was a man of valour, with a high degree of intelligence, and often advised Ashoka on matters of administration and external affairs.

King Ashoka sent a missive to Uthiyan Cheralathan for an urgent meeting. Uthiyan Cheralathan accepted the invite and immediately left for Pataliputra, capital of the Mauryan Empire. King Ashoka described the concept of the divine hands.

Since the origin of the world, various scholars had conducted many types of experiments to understand the origin of the universe. A few saints had even conducted a study on sub-atomic particles in closed chambers in the Himalayas and succeeded in formulating the concept of the origin of the universe. With their vast knowledge, they had succeeded in containing the experiment within a shell made of a hard material called *visishtam*, which was produced by heating rocks found in the Himalayan ranges and cooling it by adding certain elements to it.

The key of control for the shell lay in the valley of the Himalayas. The protection of the chambers had been entrusted to Naga sadhus, the protectors of Hindu *dharma* in this world. That tradition is alive even today in spite of the changes happening around the world.

The shell can act as an explosive and can be controlled using the key in the same way a control rod is used in a nuclear reactor. The shell and keys had been kept in different locations to avoid misuse.

Uthiyan Cheralathan took the shell back to his kingdom and kept it in the puja chamber in his palace. In the course of time, both Ashoka's and Cheralathan's dynasties declined, and Uthiyan Cheralathan's heirs formed a small kingdom called Travancore. The shell was kept safe inside the vault of their family god, Sri Padmanabha's temple in present-day Trivandrum. It stayed safe inside there escaping the local marauders like Tipu Sultan, and the ultimate looters like the British East India Company.

Chapter 8
Construction of the Vault – 1

The construction of the vault and other security measures to ensure the safety of the shell is still a mystery to the modern world. The Travancore treasury had a huge amount of gold and silver ornaments, pots and sculptures – all amassed during various conquests or offered as gifts by the kings of smaller kingdoms. It included ancient documents that could change the course of the world if they reached in the wrong hands. Hence, the heir of the treasure was not only the owner, but also the protector of mankind and the world.

The heir to this huge treasure was a descendant of Udayan Cheralathan. One day, he had a visitor from the Himalayas. A small man with a bright face in saffron clothes, the visitor came to convey a message from 'his great guruji, the emperor Ashoka', who had appeared in his dreams.

The head of the Travancore kingdom was a heavy built man with a generous smile. He was proud to be carrying the responsibility of protecting the shell and took his duty of serving the Lord Padmanabha very seriously. His main job was to ensure that no one encroached upon his country to loot the vast treasures of their land.

He asked the visitor to stay on for a few days and accept the generous hospitality of his kingdom. The visitor readily accepted the offer because he wanted to discuss some important things pertaining to the security of the world. Realizing that the visitor was tired after his long journey, the king postponed the discussions for the next day and invited him to partake of the feast at the royal dining area.

After the sumptuous dinner, the king and the visitor watched a classical dance performance. The visitor was shown into a lavish guest room with heavy wooden furniture and a beautiful sandalwood aroma.

The visitor woke up refreshed the next morning. After his morning activities and meditation, he was led into the king's conference room where the king was already seated and awaiting him.

The same pleasant sandalwood smell in the air relaxed the visitor and he came to the point immediately without much explanation. He said that he had found the emperor Ashoka sitting below a neem tree and invited the visitor to sit with him. The visitor's demeanour brought out the respect he had for his guruji as he spoke. "My guruji told me the story of the shell and the importance of protecting it. He warned me about the dangers that it could wreak on mankind if it reached the wrong hands. He requested me to visit you to discuss and find measures to protect the shell, and in turn, mankind. That is why I am here."

He continued in a soft voice, "Immediately after that, I woke up to find myself in a small room on a high mountaintop, that I realised were the Himalayas. A member of society called the nine unknown men; the visitor had left immediately on horseback to the kingdom located far away in the south. During his journey, he made a mental plan of the vault and the security measures that needed to be taken to protect it.

The king expressed his view of keeping the shell near the temple, saying that no one would ever suspect that such a thing existed and that too, inside the temple.

The king summoned one of his trusted workers to start the construction of the vault immediately without revealing what exactly would go into it. He summoned his trusted head worker and told him that he needed something to be protected from falling into the hands of the wrong people. Only three people knew the exact purpose for the construction of the vaults – the visitor, king and his trusted worker.

To the rest of the world, it was just a regular renovation of the temple during which access was denied to the public. The construction workers were told that the chamber was being constructed to protect the king from his enemies in case of an attack on the kingdom.

They selected an auspicious day to start the task and after prayers to the earth and other gods, the work started. The king arranged for a huge feast for his people to mark the importance of the day.

Chapter 9
Construction of the Vault – 2

The construction of vault started as per the plan. The materials used for its construction were unique and specially procured hard material from the eastern part of India. The solid rocks covered with molten metals made it virtually impossible to destroy. Holes were made in them to insert the iron rods for the vault. The thickness of the vault wall was more than a whole metre, making it totally impregnable by any force on earth.

The huge area dug up near the temple filled up with water and obstructed the construction site. The workers then constructed huge water wheelers operated by elephants to remove water from the pits.

Huge rocks were selected from the rocks that came in. As instructed by the visitor, the workers melted a number of metals together in a locally-made furnace. This mixture was then poured over the selected rocks. The huge basement of the vault was cast with this. Next came the thick impenetrable walls that could withstand earthquakes of high magnitude. An additional metal layer sealed the joints. The slab above the vault was cast in molten metal and put in place with the help of the elephants. Another layer of molten metal was then applied to the internal surfaces of the wall.

The next big thing was connecting the vault with the palace through an underground tunnel. The tunnel was dug manually and lined with molten metal around the circumference.

To keep the treasure accessible, the doors were made of molten metal with a lock system fixed into the walls. The doors were unique – they were hollow and filled with snakes. Any movement of the doors would create a particular frequency of sound that would make the snakes come out.

The treasure was moved in covered boxes from the palace using elephants. It took more than a hundred elephants to shift the entire treasure into the vault. The most valuable and dangerous substances were placed in the specially-designed internal cells and the less valuable items in the cells along the sides.

After all the shifting was complete, king cobras were captured and placed inside the hollow doors. The vaults were then closed with a mud mixture that would react to become rocks, if disturbed. The keys were handed over to the king, who gave them to his closest aide to keep safe.

After making sure that everything was placed in the vaults safely, the visitor left for his house in the Himalayas.

Chapter 10
Lothskid Lab, 7th October 2008

The plane carrying the treasure took off towards the Alps. The two other flights that accompanied the plane bore the NATO logo to avoid suspicion. The mercenaries sitting inside the planes were old war veterans from the various armed forces and started celebrating by pouring out drinks and playing music. Each of them had already secretly begun to count their fortunes. The leader of the group was a heavyset American with a big moustache who rarely spoke nor smiled throughout the journey.

"We will land at our destination in a few minutes from now," announced the pilot.

The plane landed at a secret base constructed in a valley in the Alps bordering Switzerland. The building near the base looked like a research facility with large boundary wall constructed around it. The mercenary group alighted from the plane one by one. The place was astoundingly beautiful with mountains on all sides.

A few people in business suits stood there to welcome them. The lady among them looked like a Hollywood actress and had just shared a joke which made all of them laugh. The leader of the mercenaries came forward to hand over the box to a strong, well-built man in a black suit.

"Did you open the box during the journey?" asked the leader of the reception committee.

"No we did not! You can trust us on that. All that we want is our payment. We're not concerned about your antiques," the leader of the mercenaries said promptly.

"Well, of course, you will receive a bonus too for a job well done!" responded the leader smiling.

"Bring out the big box, guys," he ordered his assistants.

He handed over the suitcase with millions of dollars in it. Within minutes, the mercenaries got back into the aircraft and departed – back to their mundane everyday lives – until the call for the next mission came.

The box was not opened immediately as the deal was made by the team that always carried out the missions Lothskid assigned to them all around the world. The missions included kidnapping, political killings, destabilization of the countries, extradition of leaders from conflicted areas among other things that caught Lothskid's fancy.

There was an air of curiosity in the lab as everyone awaited the opening of the box. The lady seemed particularly interested having fixed her gaze on the box ever since it had been handed over. A hush fell over the room as the box was opened….but, to everyone's astonishment, the object looked like a normal black stone without any shine. There was something carved on it in Sanskrit.

"This stone contains hell of a love mystery," said the scientist.

"It's all yours to explore and break into pieces, if needed!" said the leader.

The boss had ordered them to take the object immediately to the lab for further experiments on it. It was awaited by various equipment with their capabilities to release rays of various wavelengths and frequencies. One equipment can generate laser rays that are powerful enough to assess the nanostructure of all available solid objects on Earth.

"The Hindus – they were the real inventors of the world," the boss said in a calm voice.

Chapter 11

An unexpected invitation

Raju was sitting in his office with Upadhyay discussing the happenings in brief to find an answer to the riddles. They were still not able to understand the situation. Their conversation kept going back to the man they had met and the subsequent discussions leading nowhere – they felt they were getting transferred into a mysterious world.

"Mr. Upadhyay, What do you feel about the situation? Can we trust the man we met?"

"Sir, we don't have a choice right now but to rely on his words, even if not fully. We need some more clarifications. Also, the man needs to prove that the object does indeed exist."

"We also need to be patient," he added.

"What do you think about the death of the royal servant? It seems that the people who committed the burglary in the temple are involved. That is a forgone conclusion, don't you think?" asked the boss.

"Seems to be so, but we need to explore other options too."

"Do you mean the involvement of that politician?" asked the chief looking more interested now.

"Yes. It has been proved through our investigation that the politician was at the hotel on the day of Shankaran's death. We also found out that a huge amount of money has been transferred to the account of a company registered in the name of his wife through a national bank. We have received a copy of the Foreign Inward Remittance Certificate. Added to all this, his sudden rise in ranks so soon…. it's unbelievable!"

"Well, he was appointed cabinet minister in the energy department," added Upadhay.

"Energy…that is the word we need to focus on!" whispered the boss, making a mental note of it.

"So, what do you think about the death of the cabinet minister and the uprising in Arankulam that led to the closing of the nuclear energy project?" inquired the chief.

"Do you mean to say that the same person is involved in this too?"

"It's just a guess. Let's start with an investigation on his past bank transactions and the source of funding from the abroad. I think that could give us some kind of lead. Since the case is related to national safety and an attack by foreign forces on our soil, you have every right to go to any extent," affirmed the chief.

"Also, please maintain the secrecy of the investigation – do not disclose the purpose to anyone during the investigation. Another thing, get the CCTV video recordings of the hotel on the night of Shankaran's death. That should give us some vital clues," added the chief.

Upadhyay left the office and the chief returned to his own world of thoughts until he was interrupted by a phone call. "Could I speak to the head of investigations?"

The chief identified the voice immediately. "Yes, I was expecting your call."

"Will you be able to visit Manali, Sir? It's important," asked the voice on the other side.

"Why? What is important?"

"Because the world needs to know a secret and there's no one better than you to be the messenger for it. The world is under a huge threat," replied the voice solemnly.

"Once you agree, I will arrange the conveyance for you from Manali to our place," continued the voice.

The meeting point had been discussed, but the chief was anxious about meeting a stranger and trusting him. But since the matter was relevant to the security of the nation, he agreed to go. He left a message for his superior and told his family that he would be out of town for work for a couple of days.

Soon, he started on his journey. As promised, the vehicle had been arranged for him up to Manali. In the meantime, his aide, Upadhyay, had left for Trivandrum to carry out the job entrusted to him. Being a no-nonsense person and due to the importance of his mission, he purposely kept a distance from the others.

Chapter 12
The Lothskid Lab – 2

The lab area contained highly polished glass platforms, super computers, various powerful scanning machines and chemicals, some of which were unknown to the rest of the world. All possible measures were taken to ensure the secrecy of the operations. The scientists were hired for huge contract amounts and were provided with all facilities so that they did not have to leave the campus lab. The Lothskid had the best brains in the world for their lab operations. The lead scientist Dr. Hiroshi was hired from a university in Japan.

The stone was placed in a holder on the lab platform. The scanner had been switched on with the laser rays focused on the object with all the senior scientists in attendance. What was puzzling was that there was nothing on the screen except a black image!

Dr Hiroshi admitted to seeing such an object that could not be scanned for the first time in his life. He pondered about the possible reasons for the phenomenon, and said that he needed to explore something beyond normal intelligence. He recalled reading a book at the Oxford University library – it was the translation of an ancient Indian book titled *Arthik Samhita*. It contained details about various materials used in the field of manufacturing and inventions. Maybe he would be able to get some idea about the materials that absorbs the rays of various wavelengths. Without wasting any time, he booked a ticket to London.

The stone was kept on the platform for further testing under full security. At midnight, the security personnel heard a slow chant echoing all around the lab. Just as they were being lulled into a trance, there was a huge noise. The stone had shattered the glass! A chunk of energy had left the stone in the form of waves breaking the stone into tiny pieces.

The stone had an inbuilt mechanism that could release the stored energy in the form of controlled waves. The theory of how and why is still hidden in the vast treasure of knowledge in India. The amount of devastation during the release of extra energy could prove the intensity of explosion, if the stone had released all the energy it had inside. The stone needed to be kept inside the special box made of a special material to contain that energy.

Although Dr. Hiroshi was informed of the explosion when he was on the way to Oxford, he decided to carry on with his research to find out about the material that he couldn't scan. After a quick shower and a light breakfast, he made his way to the material science book section.

He picked out the book he had been looking for – *Arthik Samhita*. The book had a detailed description of the materials used to prepare weapons in India. It also contained details about how nuclear technology was incorporated into long range weapons to produce large scale devastation. Apart from that, there was ample information on the materials used to contain nuclear reactions. He finally found the details of a material called *visishtam*. It was produced by heating specific stones found in the Himalayas up to a certain temperature and cooling it by adding certain elements into it. The book clearly mentioned that since it was almost impossible to destroy this material, it was therefore, used as a cover for various weapons used in ancient India.

Dr Hiroshi was mesmerized by the technological advancement of ancient India. "The stone in the lab…. wonder what that is made of," he thought to himself as he flipped the pages quickly to get a clue. He felt that it was either a nuclear weapon or something that was used for experiments. In both cases, its destruction would be the same – dangerous – because it would act as a nuclear weapon that could destroy the world. He called the lab immediately to instruct the officials to transfer the stone into a chamber with hard walls.

Chapter 13
The Concept of 9 Unknown Men

The concept of the nine unknown men was first recognized by Emperor Ashoka. It says that at any given moment of time, society has nine great men who are responsible for changing the fate of the future. It is believed that scientists like Jagadish Chandra Bose received advice and information from them to change the course of science as well as the future of mankind. The accumulated knowledge was passed on from one set of members to the next, and is supposedly stored in an unknown vault somewhere in the middle of Himalayan ranges. New members are inducted into this society through the process of mutual consent. These rare geniuses are usually spotted through certain groups who have dedicated their lives to this purpose. Nowadays the group includes prominent professors, economists and a few entrepreneurs in India. There have also been some rare occurrences of inducting foreigners into this group several times.

Ancient India witnessed many wars, some of which some were catastrophic. One such war took place in 850 BCE. It marked the end of the Kaurava rule and the coming of power of the Pandavas. It is said that the large number of weapons like Brahmastra, Agneyastra, Pasupatastra, Narayanastra, Nagastra and Vayavyastra, used in the battle resembled some of our present-day nuclear bombs. The destruction and devastation they caused was powerful enough to change nature within a few seconds.

Krishna, the mastermind of the war, had a weapon called *sudharsana* that was so powerful that it could hide the sun by making changes in the atmosphere. These weapons were created by scholars who possessed deep knowledge.

The manufacturing details of the weapons were passed down through generations until the rule of Emperor Ashoka. However, after witnessing the horrible scenes of the great Kalinga war, Ashoka decided to put an end to the violence in the world and make it a place worth living. For this he invited the top nine scholars of his time to discuss how to keep the science of weapon technology a secret, and also to focus on the scientific advances for the betterment of mankind.

The secret technology that had been preserved in the form of a book was written in a script unknown to rest of the world, and was kept in the safe custody of the unknown men until now. This group of men had turned their attention from developing weaponry to using science for the betterment of mankind paving the way for all the scientific advances we see today.

Each member chose a specific subject and started researching towards improving it, and was responsible for guarding and improving his/her choice of book. Each of the books dealt with a different branch of potentially hazardous knowledge. The books cover the following subjects:

Propaganda and Psychological Warfare

This includes the preparation of propaganda and psychological means to intimidate the enemy. The initial concepts were borrowed from Chanakya's *Arthasasthra* but improvised to suit the present modes of operation of various governments and policies ruling the world. Concepts like blocking the income generation of the enemy and encouraging internal conflicts in the enemy's territory were described in detail in this book much before the worldwide use of these ideas by western powers.

Physiology

This includes instructions on how to perform the 'touch of death'. Some say that the martial art form judo is a product of the material leaked from this book. All the martial art forms in the world were devised by Buddhist scientists who learnt them from ancient India.

Microbiology

Called biotechnology in modern terms. Some versions of the myth say that the water of the Ganges has been purified with special microbes designed by the Nine Unknown Men and released into the river at a secret base in the Himalayas.

Alchemy

This includes the transmutation of metals. There is a persistent rumor in India that during times of drought or other natural disasters, temples and religious organizations receive large quantities of gold from an unknown source. The mystery is further deepened by the fact that the sheer quantity of gold in temples and with kings cannot be accounted for, considering that India has such few gold mines.

Communication

This includes communication with extraterrestrials. Ancient Indian texts like the *Vedas* and epics like the *Mahabharata* show that people could hear voices from another world.

Gravitation

The *Vaiminakasastra* is said to contain instructions that are necessary to build a *vimana* that can take off against gravity and the wind. Sometimes referred to as the ancient UFOs of India, the concept of *vimanas* is said to have originated from India, and is mentioned in the epic *Ramayana* as *pushpakavimana*, which was used by Ravana.

Cosmology

This is the capacity to travel at enormous speeds through space and time, including intra- and inter-universal trips.

Light

This is the capacity to increase and decrease the speed of light, to use it as a weapon by concentrating it in a certain direction.

Sociology

This includes the rules concerning the evolution of societies and how to predict their downfall. In ancient times, some saints were able to predict the end of *yugas* or the survival span of certain civilizations. These are mentioned in the *Vedas*.

These 9 men avoided all forms of religious, social or political association, and kept themselves concealed from the public deliberately. They were the nine incarnations of ideal men of science. They were supremely aloof, but conscious of their moral obligations. They had the power to mould the destiny of the human race, but refrained from exercising this power. This secret society is the finest tribute imaginable to the freedom of the most exalted kind. Looking down from the watchtower of their hidden glory, these nine unknown men watched civilizations being born, destroyed and re-born again, tolerant rather than indifferent, and ready to come to the rescue – but always observing that rule of silence. That is the mark of human greatness.

Chapter 14
Meeting with the 9 Unknown Men

Raju reached the designated meeting point at Manali early in the morning. He pulled the collars of his coat up to his ears to fight off the chill. He had no idea about the remaining part of the journey. The driver cum security guard was his only companion as they waited. He knew he had put himself at some risk because the voice at the other end of the phone carried a heaviness and seemed more like the answer to his labyrinth of questions. The only other person he was in touch with was his assistant Upadhay – through a small communication device secured in his pocket. He started getting restless and walked up and down a bit. Then, he lit up a Wills Navy Cut cigarette and took a deep puff.

After some time, an old vintage car stopped in front of him. An old man with in loose saffron attire got out of the car and came towards him .The old man's face was bright and confident. He had an aura of greatness surrounding his face. He invited the chief into his car to travel further to an unknown location. Raju was a little hesitant but decided to get in because he was curious and wanted answers.

The car started and they started driving through the hills towards the valley of secrets. Raju was so anxious about the destination that beads of sweat started forming on his forehead even in that cold weather. He was suddenly seized by an abnormal feeling of somnolence. He just couldn't keep his eyes open and was fast asleep in no time. The car passed through a path that offered a visual treat to the passengers, but Raju was fast asleep.

He was woken up by the old man to find a big old-fashioned house located in the middle of the mountains and reflecting the clear moonlight. As he gained consciousness, he kept feeling that he was falling into a trap of the enemy and began to curse himself for putting himself and the nation in such a risky situation.

The old man got off the car and invited him into the big house. Hesitantly, he walked in to find himself in a huge room that resembled a big workshop cum library with many machines and books in it. He was pointed towards a heavy-cushioned sofa and settled himself into it. His eyes took in the interiors as he wondered where on earth he was. The mystery was deepening and he couldn't concentrate as the chill in the air was making him drowsy.

The old man had gone inside and he could hear some whispering. Even through his drowsiness, he was assessing the area. He got the feeling that the building was occupied by more men. He was also getting a feeling of deja vu especially due to the heavenly smell he was getting.

Another man accompanied the old man outside and both of them invited Raju to join them for dinner. He was led to a room that had one electric bulb glowing. "Wonder how they got electricity to such a remote location?" he thought to himself.

There were about seven people sitting on the floor in the room. They greeted him cordially and gave him a seat amidst them. Within a minute or so, there was a hush and as he looked around, everyone in room had their eyes closed and started chanting something in pure Sanskrit. Raju quickly shut his eyes too. The menu was simple – fruits, rice and some boiled vegetables without any flavour or spices. Everyone ate in silence. Raju was offered a glass of milk after the meal. He accepted it thankfully and drank it up in one go without any hesitation.

After the unpretentious dinner, Raju was silently led to a sweet-smelling bedroom with wood panelled walls. Although he wanted answers to a lot of questions, he was unable to ask because he was too sleepy and tired.

However, the old man himself started speaking to him. "You will get all the answers to your questions in a few days. Be patient. You will understand the circumstances that have led you here. You will be emboldened to exercise some duties that will alter the fate of the world in the coming days. For now, just sleep peacefully – don't put any pressure on your mind." He then put his hand on his forehead. It was as if he was tranquilized! Raju dozed off in the calm and serene atmosphere without any disturbance from the outside world.

Chapter 15
A Wake-up Call

Raju woke up early in the morning feeling fresh face and energetic. Looking out of the window, he saw mountains covered with snow and the rising sun in a distance. The air had a fresh aroma and as he was breathing in this scene, a young man entered the room with a tray. The young man had the face of a yogi – sharp cheekbones and looking unusually calm and bright. His voice was soft, but authoritative. "Guruji is waiting for you in the garden near the front."

Raju looked around the house along his way to the outside, marveling at how the sunlight reached each and every part of the house through the carefully positioned mirrors that reflected the light from the sun. He was looking forward to meeting the other nine men he had had dinner with the previous day, but he didn't see anyone on the way to the garden.

The garden was purely natural with many plants he had never seen before. He saw many animals roaming around freely. In one corner, he noticed an old man wearing round spectacles sitting on a stone bench feeding food to the rabbits and squirrels gathered around him. The old man looked familiar – it was as if he had met him somewhere earlier, but he couldn't place him. His face and body indicated that he was over a hundred years old but his speech was clear and concise.

"Don't be surprised! You already know me although we've never had the chance to meet – I am knows as Netaji in your world."

The chief was dumbstruck.

The old man continued, "I was not killed in any air crash as you believe. I was moved here much before the incident. All the stories you heard about the plane crash were fabricated by people who didn't want me to be alive."

"But…but...for what?" spluttered the chief in shock and surprise.

"The history that you have learnt is totally fabricated. I really didn't want to spoil any images just for the sake of proving myself as the real freedom fighter."

"But at this age, everything seems like a mystery," said the chief.

"Well, I am alive and well. And I have a reason to live – to fight a war – the last war for humankind, which will happen anytime soon."

"How do you know that?" asked the chief curiously.

Netaji smiled and replied, "The fight between evil and good has been on since the origin of the world!"

The chief was at his wit's end but continued the conversation. "Why was I brought here?"

"Humanity is in danger. We wanted a person who is capable of handling the situation in a mature and wise way on our side."

"I'm still confused…what has led to such a dangerous situation?"

"Do you remember the meeting at the Padmanabha Temple in Trivandrum? The yogi has already explained to you that the shell is a potential nuclear bomb that is capable of destroying half of the earth in seconds. It has reached the hands of the wrong people. Luckily for us, they have not yet discovered the technique to detonate it. If they find it, it will wipe out the entire human race."

"There could be a war while retrieving the shell from the wrong hands too," said the chief.

"The final war is meant for the bravest people," said Netaji.

"What will my role be in this war?"

"With time, you will know everything, because you will join us in the fight."

"How long I will have to be here?"

"About a week. You will know the entire plan by then."

"Anything else in store for me?"

"Yes! You will know about a tradition, the nine unknown men, who will decide the fate of the world from now on," responded the charismatic leader.

Chapter 16

Narendra - The Young Man

After his *sattvik* breakfast of fruits and some grains with milk, Raju took a walk with the young man he had met in the morning, around the garden.

"Where is everyone? I don't see anyone here," the chief started the conversation after assessing the young man for some time with an investigating officer's eye.

"They left for the lab early this morning, and will return in the afternoon," The young man responded.

"What sort of experiments are they doing?"

"Anything that benefits the human race as a whole – that makes an impact on humankind for generations to come."

"But how is the outside world benefitting from these experiments?"

"They have disciples all over through whom the benefits of the experiments are reaching the world."

"What do you do here?"

"I was recruited by these people for a higher purpose – to lead the nation in the future, to become the leader of a political party, to lead the country to its spiritual and cultural peak, one that we left behind about two hundred years ago."

"But is that even possible? We have already reached a stage where moral and cultural values have come down to the lowest possible level."

"Everything is possible! You are right about these values having come down, but there is still a spark in the mind of the younger generation. One just needs to ignite it with the flow of correct knowledge and through spiritual motivation."

"But how can this be done?"

"The education system needs to be changed. There needs to be more focus on the spiritual awakening within human beings rather than evoking a competitive mindset in them. One needs to understand himself first, then the nature and fellow beings around him, and then their coexistence. Our current educational system is somewhat of a mental torture - one that lessens the capacity of a human being to think even though it improves memory. They are forced to think only in a particular way. It makes for a subjugated mind that can be conquered very easily. This just increases the competition between people rather than stimulating mutual trust and cooperation. All the people who do not obey rules and systems are either outcast or become failures at a later stage."

"So how do you plan to implement these plans right now?"

"First, by improving people's confidence and self-esteem. Their minds need to start challenging all the things that are not acceptable to them. They are living a clueless life imitating celebrities and false idols without realizing the hidden potential lying within them. The purpose of living lies in actualizing the inborn abilities one is blessed with.

"May I know your name? Sorry for not asking it till now," said the chief admiring the young man.

"Narendra."

"One more thing – how do you plan to clean up the existing corrupt political system?"

"Anything that is baseless will get destroyed on its own. The youth will soon realize that the opinions and prejudices imposed on their subconscious minds without their knowledge. Do you think that they will adjust with the restrictions imposed on them by the current system any further? Within them lies the power to fire the world with the correct knowledge and unlimited abilities – and that will be unleashed in a short time. We just need to wait and witness the awakening within them; the final awakening that will destroy all the lies and false knowledge that is making them feeble victims," the young man's voice was trembling with anger.

He asked the chief, "Do you know anything about the precious things that our forefathers left us for our wellbeing?"

The chief frowned hearing the young man's answer.

"It is the wisdom, the conventional wisdom, the abundance of knowledge, the knowledge that ranged from trigonometry to rocket science. But we fools have forgotten ourselves in the flow of unrealistic knowledge. People have started despising their own culture, language and the real knowledge. Everything was imposed upon them in the form of bad music, worthless culture and the way of living through the television channels and films. The worst thing is that nobody is even trying to know what is happening to them anymore," responded the young man in anger.

"How do you expect to bring about a change??" asked the chief.

"Simple! Through an educational system that teaches the right thing at the right time," replied the young man firmly. "The gurus of the future are getting ready at our lab to bring about the required changes in society by imparting the real knowledge to the youth."

Chapter 17

The Nine Unknown Men's Lab

The chief was asked to visit the lab in which the experiments were being conducted by the nine unknown men. The lab was located in a serene place a few furlongs away from the house. They had to cross a river on a bamboo and rope bridge to reach it.

It was made of natural materials like wood and various other materials invented by the nine unknown men to be in sync with the surrounding environment. Although the walls of the lab were transparent, they were soundproofed and provided a fabulous view of the scenic environment. The structure had undergone numerous changes with the passage of time to accommodate the latest experimental requirements and testing for the materials developed by the nine unknown men. It resembled a natural forest with many small trees and plants inside it. It even had some animals wandering about inside.

The nine unknown men conducted several experiments on various subjects in this lab, and recorded the process and results both in physical form as well as through data kept for the use of generations to come. It had a central atrium to conduct open space experiments.

The nine unknown men were assisted by some young men recruited from all over the world. A few of them were going to become a part of the nine unknown men of the next generation.

The crucial experiments were conducted inside specially constructed areas and there were advanced arrangements to change the entire environment as per the requirements. The hazardous areas were specially constructed and isolated from rest of the areas. A room in the corner had a super computer with a high level of computational capacity. The lab was conducting many advanced experiments to bring a change to the existing systems or processes.

They entered the area being used for astronomical, cosmic, extra-terrestrial and communication experiments. The chief was astounded with the huge array of experiments being carried out there. Many of these were beyond the grasp of normal human beings and was highly classified so that there was no misuse.

The nine unknown men disclosed only those results that would benefit humanity without making any abrupt changes. Theirs was not to disrupt the existing socio-ecosystems, beliefs and nature.

Raju was then led into a meeting chamber where the nine unknown men and Netaji were already seated and waiting for him to discuss their future course.

Chapter 18
The Mission

Upadhay reached the Trivandrum airport early in the guise of a businessman from the northern part of India. Being part of the high profile investigation agency, he had high observation skills and could easily disguise himself as he wished. He had stayed the night at a nearby hotel instead of the guest house meant for government officials.

He had booked a ticket to Arankulam and was joined by two other officers also posing as businessmen. They reached the village in the afternoon and checked into the only hotel in the area, posing as realtors wanting to invest in the area. They were told to contact one of the leaders of the agitation, who invited them to his house for a discussion and apprised them of the prospective developments there. Upadhyay and his colleagues showed that they were interested in investing in the region mainly because of the plant slated to come up there.

The leader hesitated in replying to their query on the plant, but when the officials offered him a partnership, he looked interested. They invited him to the hotel for further discussion on it later that evening.

They started the discussion over a drink and a suitcase with five lakh rupees as an advance. Enthused by the offer, the leader started to disclose the details of the possible obstruction to the commencement of the plant operations. The drinks loosened his tongue a little and he told him about the involvement of the political powers in the entire course of events. He had no idea that the conversation was being secretly recorded as proof for the investigation.

They came back to Trivandrum to the hotel in which the meeting had taken place a few months ago. Their investigations revealed the information of the all people who attended the meeting –the locals, who were members of some prominent NGOs operating in India and were known to have protested against the setting up of nuclear power plants in the country with the help of Russia.

The officials embarked on their journey to Bangalore to the headquarters of the NGOs. They sought the help from the income tax department officials for conducting the raids. The investigation officers posed as tax officials and the whole operation was projected as a normal income tax raid conducted without much hype and media coverage. The seized documents included details of huge sums of donations received from a company headquartered in London. The company dealt with global energy technology solutions.

On the way to the airport, Upadhyay and his team were waylaid by a group of foreigners who looked like stranded tourists seeking help. The driver was dragged out of the car and held captive as the mercenaries pulled out AK-47s from their bags and aimed them at the officials. They had been hired again to strike on the officials, who unbeknownst to them had been monitored continuously after the recent raid. But just before they could press the triggers, the foreigners were shot down by a volley of bullets. The group of persons approached the vehicle cautiously, then quickly piled up the bodies inside their vehicle. Introducing themselves as *suryavanshis*, the warriors of the great god Surya, they told the terrified Upadhyay and his team that they had instructions from their chief to protect them. Their chief, they said, was closely associated with the nine unknown men. They had long faces with sharp jaws and wore tattoos of the lord Surya on their foreheads. After making sure that the officials reached the airport safely, they went back to their hideout.

Chapter 19

The Legend of the *Suryavanshis*

The Sun Temple at Konarak was built around 1250 AD by the East Ganga king Narasimhadeva. The administration of temple was handled by the Suryavanshis and their families. Built of stone, the temple had stones and iron rods which were kept in position by two powerful magnets placed right at the top. The magnets not only kept the stones in place, but also made the deity inside the sanctum sanctorum hover. The temple was built in such a way that the morning sun touched the feet of the deity at the start of the day. Even today, it is possible to calculate time by placing a finger on the axis of the wheel sculptured around the temple.

A long time ago, a ship washed ashore. Its passengers were mainly white-skinned people who had business relations with small kingdoms in the subcontinent. The foreigners mingled with the locals and adapted to their culture and life. They were very interested in the temple and its architecture. But it was the hovering deity that attracted them the most. It was a huge wonder.

After spending many long days there, they returned to their native land located far away. Soon, more and more ships started coming ashore, and the natives started getting used to them. They started becoming familiar with the foreigners and developed business dealings with them too.

However, the natives were taken unawares when one fine sunny morning, the white-skinned people returned with ships loaded with cannons and other artillery, and began to fire indiscriminately at the temple. They were aiming at the place the magnets were supposed to be located. One group got off their ship with guns and swords, and started moving towards the temple.

The locals and the priests assembled with whatever weapons they had, but were unable to withstand the heavily armed invaders. They entered the sanctum sanctorum, but the deity was missing! They started looting the temple and took away whatever valuables they could find back to the ship. But the captain of the ship was not satisfied – he refused to return without the hovering deity.

He rounded up all the women and the children of the village and started threatening to kill them all till he got the deity he had come for. The chief priest had taken it away to hide it in a safe place. He ran back home and instructed his wife and kids to leave the place immediately. He whispered something in his eldest child's ears and left without looking back. The family managed to escape through the bushes behind their home.

The priest handed over the deity to the captain, who accepted it with a smile and fired a bullet into the priest's chest. He instructed his men to kill all the assembled women and children and take some of the women captive to their ship. They then ransacked the entire village and burnt it down.

Destroying the temple was not as easy as looting the village. They aimed the cannons to the top of the temple, but were not able to damage it because the strong magnets deflected the bullets. So they started melting iron objects together and made a cannon ball with it. The ball was then fired into the magnet. This displaced the alignment of the magnets and soon the temple was destroyed. Their mission accomplished, the white-skinned people quickly got back into their ships and left the place.

In the meantime, the priest's family had travelled along the forests and reached a hill, where they met a saint. The saint had come from Himalayas and settled there. He imparted all forms of knowledge including weaponry skills to children to help them to survive in the world. One day without saying anything to anyone, he went back to his abode in the Himalayas. The priest's family settled down there. And thus started the saga of the Suryavanshis whose sole objective was to bring back the lost idol.

The saint was one of the nine unknown men who was fond of travelling around the world and learning new things. Unknown to the rest of the world, a special bond was made between two groups, the Suryavanshis and the nine unknown men.

Chapter 20
When a big tree falls…

When Upadhay and his team reached the capital, they were greeted by the media. As per instructions of the chief, they handed over copies of the documents to them. The chief thought it was better to expose the politician through the media to avoid the complications that were likely if they proceeded the official way.

Upadhay placed the original copies of the documents in a secure vault in his office and came home to rest for the day. By the time he woke up in the afternoon, all the news channels were flashing the minister's role in sabotaging one of the country's most prestigious energy projects and the alleged transactions with the foreign entities. The opposition picked up the news immediately and soon there were huge protests asking the minister to resign.

By that time, the chief had returned to Delhi and called for a press conference to reveal certain hidden secrets. He had all the documents related to the theft of the shell and the involvement of the politician, and wanted to reveal the various anti-national activities that posed a threat to mankind. Although the chief was a bit nervous about the details he was going to present, he knew he had to do it considering the safety of his nation and country.

He narrated the whole story starting from the death of the Travancore palace assistant and the involvement of the politician in the uprising that took place in Arankulam; and the theft of one of the most valuable items from the temple. He told them about the shell and how it could be controlled, and about the potential threat to the nation because of its theft. He gave details about the controlling mechanism of the shell mentioning that the controlling key was hidden in a secret place guarded by the Naga sadhus. He was careful not to disclose anything about the precise location of the key considering national security.

He spoke about the involvement of a foreign agency in all the incidents including the death of the cabinet minister, and then stated that they were still in the process of looking for proof for people involved in the temple burglary and details of the flight movement.

Far away from the boundaries of the nation, there were some equally curious ears picking up the latest developments in India, which could also affect them.

The revelations caused huge outrage against the politician all around the country. The prime minister called for an urgent meeting in which he forced the minister to resign. He did not want to take a risk from any kind of agitation that would shake up his ministry.

Within a few hours, the ousted minister was taken into custody. The chief was satisfied with the events, but knew that he had a lot left to do. The hard work had paid off, he thought to himself as he lay down for the much-needed rest.

Besides exposing the minister, the chief had a another reason for his preplanned press conference. He was waiting for a reaction from the people involved.

And that was exactly what happened. Within a couple of hours, he received the expected phone call –from a location far away from India.

"Hi chief!" said the voice on the other end of the phone. He returned the greeting calmly, determined to face the future course of events.

"Congratulations for the recent achievement," said the voice, which seemed to have something more in his mind. "Thanks for calling. How can I help you?" he asked, although he knew exactly why he had called.

The voice on the other end offered him a huge amount of money for revealing the location of the control key and further growth in the political arena. Since the chief was expecting the offer, he knew what he had to say. He paused for a minute and then responded by saying that he would accept the offer on two conditions.

The first was to take him to the place where the shell was being kept, and the second was to gift him the hovering deity of Konarak that was stored in a private museum in London.

When the voice asked him the reasons for his conditions, the chief said, "Personal interests."

The voice paused and after some time asked for a day to confirm.

Within a day, the chief got a call from a different number. They had agreed to his conditions. The very next day, the chief resigned from his post as head of NIA.

Chapter 21

Lothskid Lab - 3

The chief was ready for a journey that was going to be a turning point his life.

A man in a black suit walked up to him and introduced himself as a well-wisher. The chief was waiting at the airport for the Lothskid Lab agent to accompany him to Dubai from Delhi. They went through security and climbed into the waiting chartered flight. They flew towards a private airport located near the Lothskid Lab. The facilities in the plane were 5-star quality replete with charming airhostesses. Soon after take-off, they offered exquisite liquor and snacks. The chief politely declined the alcohol, but asked for some of the delectable snacks on offer. By the time they reached their destination, it was late at night.

The chief was taken to the resort near the lab and guided to his room – with expensive wooden furniture and electronics. He took a bath and opened a prayer book to calm himself down.

He woke up early the next day and practised yoga for a few hours before breakfast. He was then guided into a serene area full of plants. The chief stood there waiting for his hosts to come.

The host was an old man who came bang on time with Dr. Hiroshi to meet the chief. He was dressed in an elegant suit and looked very serious.. He greeted the visitor with a smile and asked about the recent developments in India and spoke about his last visit to India as a tourist.

He suddenly changed the topic and asked, "What on earth made you change your mind about handing over the information to us?"

"The same thing that you are after. Money and power."

"I will not able to make even a quarter of what you offered working lifelong in that organization," he added.

"Well, you've made a fantastic decision and I congratulate you."

"The funds will be transferred to your account in a foreign bank."

"That's very nice of you. Thank you. But what about my other two conditions?" asked the chief.

"We have taken those conditions seriously and have already brought it from the museum," the old man answered, and gestured to one of his men to bring the idol.

When the man brought the idol in a black leather bag, the chief physically examined the idol. "I have a deep connection with this and request you to let me keep it until I go back to my country," said the chief.

"Of course – it's all yours! What about our condition of disclosing the location of the key?" he asked in return.

"I can take you there in person," said the chief.

"Tell us about the location and my mercenaries will bring it for me. I hope you know that you will not be freed from here until we get that," added the old man.

The chief switched on his laptop and shared the details with the old man. The old man called his team and verified the location using the advanced satellite locating system exclusively made for Lothskid. Satisfied by seeing the location, the old man turned to Dr Hiroshi to take the chief on a tour of the lab to show him the shell. No one noticed the chief carrying the black bag with the idol.

Dr. Hiroshi was a soft spoken and also spoke very little. However, he told the chief about his ongoing experiments on the shell and how impressed he was with the ancient Indian experiments and their contribution to the world. Although he listened to everything, the chief was building a plan of his own in his mind.

Chapter 22

The Strike from Nowhere

They entered the huge lab and walked straight towards the high-security vault. The heavy doors parted after the scanner recognised Dr Hiroshi's face. They entered the vault and the chief got his first glimpse of the box in which shell was kept. Without any warning, he pulled out a small pin and pressed it into the back of Dr. Hiroshi's neck to insert a sophisticated chip on him. This turned Dr Hiroshi into a being controlled from afar – from the house of the nine unknown men!

All that was happening in the lab was now visible to the nine unknown men through the high intensity radar-satellite system installed atop a peak in the Himalayas. The chip had a controlling device invented by one of the nine unknown and it used the principle of producing signals that resembled natural electrical signals transmitted by neurons.

The box carrying the shell was taken from its position and kept in the bag in which chief was carrying the idol. Suddenly, there was a booming sound in a frequency that made it difficult for humans to bear and made them lose consciousness immediately. Everyone, including the heavily armed security guards lost consciousness.

Since the chief was wearing earplugs, he was not affected and neither was Dr. Hiroshi, because he was already in a controlled mode. He guided the chief through the doors into the outer area where they found a UFO-type of object waiting for them. It was hovering in the sky and was the source of the noise that made the people faint. The saucer-like object was using the Earth's gravitational forces and solar power energy to hover on the surface. It was invented by one of the members of the nine unknown men and was being controlled remotely from the location by changing the intensity of energy consumed.

The object could float in the air and reach any height within the gravitational field in a vertical path, perpendicular to the Earth's surface unlike conventional flights. It could also traverse long distances in a shorter time than ultrasonic flights.

The object came close to the ground to allow the chief and Dr Hiroshi to climb into it. They took off and started flying towards the Himalayas.

The chief's host, the old man and his assistants at the resort had no idea about what was happening because they too had become unconscious with the loud noise.

The chief watched the entire incident with the other men through the screen located in the controlling chamber. The man sitting inside the object was actually one of the nine unknown men who had changed his appearance to that of the chief using high-end facial muscle transformation through protein substitutes and natural identical cells.

The men alighted from the object and went into the house. The man carrying the bag was in a jovial mood after his successful mission and met his colleagues and the chief inside the house. The other person inside the room was the head of *suryavanshis* waiting to take back the idol lost long ago.

After celebrating their victory, they all decided to part until the next day to make the plan for the next course of action. They needed to plan to counter the big attack headed their way to the place the controlling keys were located.

They knew that this time the blow would be massive and very advanced and needed to anticipate what the enemy would do because they could strike from anywhere. The location was purposely disclosed to the old man heading Lothskid so that the attackers came in full force. Netaji and the nine unknown men had planned an elaborate strategy to counter the attacks and neutralize the mercenaries subsequently.

Chapter 23
The Planning in Lothskid Lab

Unable to cope with the double loss, the head of Lothskid planned a huge attack to retrieve the lost things. The head of the mercenaries arrived with two of his best men to create the plan. Together, they started planning for the biggest attack they had ever carried out. For the first time again, they decided to use technology.

On the huge screens, they could see the location of the key and the present location of the shell. "Considering the geography of the location, it will be difficult to land a plane there. And since the land is uneven, carrying out an attack immediately after landing will be disastrous. So we need to think of another way. Also, the place that the shell is being kept is not guarded," said the head of the mercenaries.

"Is there any information about the type of weapons these people in scanty clothes possess?" asked the chief pointing to the Naga sadhus.

"They use bows and arrows, and swords," he laughed.

"Never undermine them…I made a mistake once! They used technologies that are still in the experimental stages in our labs," said the old man.

"That is a cause of concern, isn't it?" replied the head of the mercenaries.

"We will plan the attacks in multiple stages rather than a single blow," he added.

"That's a perfect plan. Sort of a blitzkrieg," whispered the old man.

"Here is a better plan – we will first use drones to carry out the attacks on the guards. By the time the drones finish the attack, about 50 of us will land on the runway located a few miles away and reach the place on snow bikes to take it further. The attacks will be carried out simultaneously at both locations."

"Make that 200. Nobody can predict the defensive technologies those bastards use," the old man said cautiously.

"And I have planned something else too. I am bringing some reinforcements from China through a beloved friend," said the old man excitedly. "These trained commandos from China will join you to protect you from any surprises. Some of them will accompany you back up to the carrier flight once you take the key, while some will guard the runway so that you are not distracted from your mission." The old man seemed to have planned everything in advance. I just need to talk to the command head of the Chinese army serving in the Himalayan regions once," said the old man.

"One more thing, please make sure that all the mercenaries wear ear muffs to protect themselves from fainting from the loud sound that will be created."

After going over the plans once again, they dispersed to arrange the resources for the final attack.

Chapter 24

The Village of Warriors

The small village located near the valley of secrets attracted warriors many various communities to settle there as instructed by the older members of the nine unknown men. It was a calm village with paddy fields and plants bearing fruits and vegetables. The village was guarded by mountains on all sides and remains unknown to the world even now.

The members included people of both sexes from all over the country, like martial arts experts – the *chekavars* from Kerala who were experts in Kalaripayattu; members of the Rajput community and the nagas; abandoned Sikh warriors and other warrior clans from all over the country.

While the male members mainly focused on weaponry training, the females worked in the fields, did crafts and made clothes for the men. The nine unknown men guided the villagers on how to grow crops in the region that had such a harsh climate.

They used weapons that were designed by the nine unknown men, and were used mainly for defence rather than assault. The village was headed by Ashwathama, who lived inside a cave close to the village for many years.

He was the same Ashwathama who had been cursed by Lord Krishna to survive in the world with a wound on his forehead for thousands of years. He came out occasionally to train the people in using some of his weapons, some of which had been replicated by the nine unknown men out of enthusiasm and zeal for ancient technology.

Affectionately called Baba, Ashwathama was a tall man at 12 feet. He spoke a rough language that nobody understood and always had a sad expression that reflected the weight of his sins committed in the past. He wanted to leave his material body at the earliest to liberate his soul. However, as a warrior, he was still strong and the way he imparted training to the members of the village proved that his skills had not worn out with the passage of time. Under his training, the warriors were known to be among the finest in the world and could combat any modern forces.

His food came from the village. The villagers made sure that he was fed before they ate.

Baba occasionally went out to meet the nine unknown men to discuss things related to ancient weaponry as he too was interested in the science behind the weapons. Sometimes, he would climb to the peak to meditate undisturbed for days to please his master Lord Shiva to forgive his sins and free his soul from this material world.

Life in the village was peaceful. Occasionally groups of Naga sadhus visited the village for food and other things. All the people living there had a simple aim – to protect the nine unknown men who would very soon become the torchbearers for humanity.

The village children learnt how to handle weapons from a very young age and became masters by the time they grew up enough to lead a family life. The community had high regard for the nine unknown men and was ready as soon as they got a call from them.

They were greeted by Netaji and the nine unknown men, and were told about their task. Together they began to chalk out the plan for the counter attack immediately. The village had about 300 men, excluding children and the old, who were trained in warfare. In addition there was a gang of Naga sadhus already protecting the area in which the key was kept.

They did not involve any external forces so that their secret remained hidden to the outside world. They did not want to break the traditions that had been followed for centuries. Added to that was the pledge taken by the nine unknown that they would never create or invent anything that would harm living beings on Earth.

They knew that they had to form a defence that would analyse the enemy's movement and neutralize them without bringing causing too much harm. They decided that the entire area would be put under surveillance using their advanced radar-satellite system. Another plan was to diffuse the enemy's electronic instruments enemy using high-frequency electrical waves. Two hundred people would cover the area including the house and lab, while the remaining would fight along with the sadhus to protect the key. They would all wear the special weapons and armour designed by the nine unknown, mainly for defence rather than attack. They wanted minimum casualties or nothing on both sides…they wanted to avoid bloodshed at any cost. The plan was to start the very next day by observing and neutralizing the enemy movement, to avoid any delays.

Suddenly, the door opened and the head of the *suryavanshis* came in to the meeting. He was invited by one of the nine unknown men, and promised to bring another hundred highly skilled warriors along with him to guard the shell and to pay for the action of bringing back their precious idol from the foreign land. To him that was the chance to take revenge on the enemy who had ransacked the village of his ancestors.

Chapter 25

The Chinese Angle

The old man made a phone call to the People's Republic of China to speak with one of his best friends in the business, a person who had helped him in various defence dealings. His friend was the commander of the army's ground force and maintained good relations with him. The old man had helped him with various weapons and defence technology business deals earlier.

The commander controlled the ground forces of the Chinese army and had the power to mobilize trained commandos to various parts of the world citing national security reasons. He had an excellent command over many languages having completed his formal education abroad like the others who held the highest positions in the Chinese communist regime.

The old man greeted him in perfect Chinese. Before diving into the matter at hand, they had a casual conversation on various things. Then, to put stress on the subject, the old man spoke in a serious voice. He narrated the whole story without a break and stressed the importance of the shell lying in the hands of a potential enemy to not only his own land, but also to the People's Republic of China.

Initially, the commander did not seem to be convinced, but later believed him. The passivity of the existence of such an object is definitely possible if the matter is connected to ancient India, he thought to himself.

He requested the old man to send some proof of the existence of such a shell. Within minutes, he had received the video footage of the things that happened in the lab.

The commander watched the video incredulously and decided to teach those Indians a lesson to safeguard his nation. He decided to get the best-trained personnel for the mission, but had to present the matter to the general before doing so. Then again, for that he would have to inform him about the most destructive weapon lying across the border with the enemy.

The next day, he presented the matter to his boss who approved it after hours of discussions. He agreed to send two groups of highly skilled commandos to assist the removal of the most threatening weapons from the enemy to safeguard their country. The two groups were composed of about 70 heavily armed commandos capable of carrying out dangerous missions in adverse climatic conditions on any terrain.

The commander called the old man back to inform him about the commandos. They decided that the mercenaries hired would also be sent to China for a few weeks for training. The leader of the mercenaries initially had some reservations about working with the Chinese, but the old man managed to convince him to go with a promise of billions of dollars and the entire expense of the operation for engaging in such a mission.

Within a few days the mercenaries moved to a secret place in the Indo-Chinese border. The Chinese welcomed them warmly.

✧ ✧ ✧

Chapter 26

The Naga Babas

Deep inside the forests of the Himalayas live the Naga babas. They never come out of this area except during the Kumbh Melas. Having dedicated their lives to the great yogi Lord Shiva, they pray for the betterment of mankind by removing negativity that surrounds the material world.

As protectors of the concept of Hindutva, the Naga sadhus go to any extent to protect the *sanatana dharma*. They believe in attaining moksha through difficult yoga postures and self-inflicted pain. They believe in the renunciation of material activities to achieve moksha. Some of them are known to possess supernatural powers, but do not use them for any destructive activities.

Many people believe that the Naga sadhus eat human flesh, practice necrophilia and extreme black magic activities, but these are just conjecture. In the likelihood of a calamity that can harm humanity, they are known to come together to take countermeasures to protect people from coming to any harm.

Baba Ranga emerged from his meditative state after foreseeing dangerous incidents that were to affect some of his men. He knew that he had to lend his support to them immediately. He quickly assembled a group of men in the forest and told them about what he had foreseen. "I saw some vultures hovering around our fellow men that are protecting the shell. They seemed to have been fighting heavily armed unknown enemies. I think my dream was a warning from Lord Shiva about the potential war. It is our duty to extend our solidarity to our men."

The group of men agreed with a roar. "*Alak niranjan,* anything to protect the interests of Lord Shiva and our fellow men!" They started preparing immediately to go to the area in which the shell was kept. They stopped in a cave on their way to retrieve their weapons. All their weapons were kept inside caves or tree trunks during peace time. They recovered weapons that had never be seen by mankind – impact resistant shields, spears, various types of bows and arrows with different type of heads.

They continued their journey with the selfless aim of protecting their fellowmen. By the evening they had reached the shore of a big lake and decided to rest for a while there. They took a bath in the chilled water and some of them entered into a meditative state.

Chapter 27
The Deployment

The Naga sadhus are said to be equivalent to some of the most elite existing commando forces in the world in terms of warfare. Their planning as well as their fighting acumen was exquisite. The lab and the house were protected by around 200 people from the village of warriors and the *suryavanshis*. The area had radar surveillance to detect movement and jammers that were installed to diffuse electronic instruments.

The nine unknown men had planned something else to avoid unnecessary bloodshed and devastation. The Naga sadhus were ready with their weapons and were prepared to sacrifice their lives to protect humanity. They had no fear and the thought of the upcoming fight did not make any impact on them at all.

The core group surrounded the location, while some others were deployed in the front of the cave to resist the assault. The rest were positioned a little distance away so as to use the long-range weapons against the enemy. The barriers supplied by the nine unknown men were placed in the front and inside the cave to resist bullets and explosives.

The sadhus kept shouting *alak niranjan, alak niranjan* from time to time to keep themselves motivated. A few of them had set up camp and started cooking for the team since they were located a couple of miles away from the house of the nine unknown men and the village.

The warriors practiced using the weapons designed by the nine unknown men. They were mainly used to unarm the enemy by affecting their senses rather than causing them physical injury. There were weapons that could be used to kill or protect themselves during assaults. The protective jackets were light but strong enough to protect them from high speed bullets or high-scale explosions. They wore matching transparent shields on their faces.

They warriors were cheerful at having being given a chance to serve the nine unknown men and humanity after a long time. The *suryavanshis* were inside the house and the lab and were armed with light assaultive weapons to neutralize enemies.

The other arrangements in the area included an automatic missile launching system that detects and destroys any means of air attack. The buildings and lab were covered with high intensity laser beam-producing equipment to ward off air attacks.

However, all these elaborate arrangements were also being noted by the enemies through their GPS. Seeing the preparedness made them rethink their air attacks. In any case, they were worried about the piling of debris over the shell which would make it difficult to retrieve. It also told them that they had to avoid any suspicion from the Indian security forces.

The *suryavanshis* had already decided to take revenge on the people who had stolen their deity and ruined the village of their forefathers.

Netaji and the nine unknown men were calm. It was just another regular day for them – they were not worried about the upcoming war. Their disciples had shifted to the village of the warriors. They had planned something big to surprise the enemy on the fateful day of the fight.

Meanwhile, the enemy camp was undergoing intense training. They were using maps and GPS images to arrive at a perfect plan that would materialize without consuming much time.

Their endurance training started early in the morning on the profile covered with thick snow. They wore the advanced life jackets used by the Chinese army, and used the latest assault weapons available. They practiced walking in the snow with their heavy gear as they had to traverse a long distance on the snowy paths up the mountain top. They practiced aiming and hurling grenades, hand-to-hand combat and riding snow bikes at high speed.

The team consisted of sniffer dogs that could attack enemies with lightning speed. The training continued for about a month. Soon, both teams were ready to carry out the mission together, although it took a long time for the Chinese to be able to interact freely with the outsiders.

The satellite photos of the area were carefully analyzed and the land profile was recreated on a mini scale. The development in the enemy area was also being watched through high-resolution satellite cameras and a live model of the war front was developed to make the perfect attack plan.

They decided to use the latest high capacity helicopters developed by the Chinese to transport the forces to the required area. The helicopters were capable of flying at a high altitude and could accommodate 60 persons at one time. The snow bikes as well as the rest of the things were transported by the dozen helicopters. There was no problem in doing so as the location was close to the Chinese border in an area not protected by the Indian forces.

They had identified a suitable location for landing using the GPS photos and division of troops to carry out the attacks in both locations. The initial assaulters and supporters were identified for the attack, and the demo attack had been practiced on the full-scale model of the enemy's area continuously for a week.

On the final day, the assaulters climbed aboard the helicopters. They started their journey at noon and were expected to reach enemy territory late at night – the perfect time to carry out a secret mission of this nature.

Chapter 28

The Final Assault

Both sides were ready for the war that would change the course of the world if the wrong side won. Although both sides looked confident, they also knew that it was not easy to win the final battle. The grip on their weapons tightened, as they thought about the glory of winning such a war. One side was motivated with money, while for the other, it was just concern for the world and humanity.

In the history of the world, there have been countless fights over many causes. These have changed the face of the world in which we live. The fights have not been bloodshed and death, they were more like writing the glorious story of the winners. If we analyse history, it is only the winners that are declared as men with good hearts. The losing side is always projected as the evil-doer.

The helicopters moved between the mountains that shone in the bright white light of the moon. The outside scene relaxed the tension of the people sitting inside the helicopters.

The helicopters landed in the pre-decided place around 10 pm. In the meantime, the mercenaries and about 150 armed commandos from the Chinese side boarded the snow bikes carrying the weapons with high-scale assaulting capabilities. They were so determined and stone-like in their cause of retrieving the shell that they could almost smell their victory.

On the other side, the men became alert after detecting the movement of the enemy within their periphery. The entire movement was being monitored on a screen inside the nine unknown men's house.

The warriors started getting ready for the tasks they had been entrusted with. But the nine unknown men had something else on their mind. If they succeeded, this fight would be a landmark in human history.

The moment the attackers crossed an unmanned barricade, their confidence level got a boost. They were sure of winning. The first team reached their destination and they stopped their snow bikes and got ready to attack.

Far away from there, the drones approached the cave. The moment the drones started shooting at the protection force inside the cave, the missionaries moved into the cave to retrieve the key. The combined force of the Naga sadhus and the warriors put up a great resistance to the intruders. The protective forces were no longer able to shield themselves using their defence mode so they swiftly switched over to their attack mode. There was a volley of bullets between the drones and the attackers. Soon, the attacking side started dominating the fight and within a couple of minutes the number of defenders declined in the volley of bullets.

All the barricades were destroyed one after another until the commandos reached the entrance of the house in which the shell was kept. The *suryavanshis* on guard inside tried to resist, but could not withstand the fierce onslaught of the commandos. They reached the room in which the nine unknown men and Netaji were and pointed their guns to their heads. The attackers managed to get to the key of the greatest weapon ever made in the history of mankind. They quickly returned to the area where the helicopters were waiting for them.

The commandos took the nine unknown men captive and pushed them into the waiting helicopters. They abandoned their further plans as they had already succeeded in achieving their main target. The doors of the helicopters closed and they took off.

And just as suddenly as everything started, all the commandos fell asleep! The cabin area was filled with a calmness, until they woke up to something unbelievable.

Chapter 29

The Unexpected

The commandos couldn't believe their eyes. Some of them shook their heads in disbelief thinking that they were still dreaming. They found themselves in a big hall with their hands and legs tied firmly with ropes, and surrounded by those they had fought the previous night. They were unable to move from the sleeping position and each one of them felt an uneasiness in their heads. "How on earth can this be possible?" they wondered.

Suddenly the nine unknown men, Netaji and the chief entered the room. They asked the commandos to calm down. "You will all be released very soon."

Unbeknownst to them, the commandoes were all under the influence of a new invention of the nine unknown men – the epitome of mental warfare. The untouched arena in any type of warfare. The very peaceful invention from the soil of the Ganges. Any war could be won without bloodshed or death.

The moment the commandos crossed the boundaries set up by the nine unknown men, they were mentally under the control of the men with magical fingers!

The commandos were under the illusion of attacking the enemy and the entire fighting drama was a programme inserted into their mind the by the nine unknown men.

The commandos were actually in a sleeping position when they were visualizing themselves in the attack. That was the invention to control the masses through virtual programming feeds into their mind through controlled electronic waves.

"Untie their legs," said one of the nine unknown to the warriors. He instructed some of the mercenaries to walk to the helicopters and freed there. The mercenaries entered the helicopters hardly believing what was happening to them. They were on their way home!

In the meantime, the other mercenaries who lay tied on the floor were wondering about their future. To their surprise, they were fed good food and water and instructed to relax in the big hall.

Just as the nine unknown men, Netaji and the chief were discussing how to prevent further attacks, Ashwathama entered the room saying that he had a better plan to put an end to all future attacks.

"What is your plan? And how can we execute it?" asked Netaji in all sincerity.

Ashwathama laughed, "The plan will be what happened after the great battle of Kurukshetra. This time the attack will be for the good side."

The people in the room could hardly digest his words as it was against their policy of non-violence. But Ashwathama convinced them that it would be his last mission and that he would retire from this world as the tenure of the curse was going to be over.

He had dreamt of a volcano in the Alps and would jump into its crater to put an end to the long life he was forced to live on this Earth. He had made a plan to visit the lab and ransack it just as he had done with the camps of the Pandavas after the great battle of Kurukshetra.

The head of the mercenaries called the old man and told him that they would return with the shell and the key to the Lothskid Lab.

The old man was frustrated as he was not able to get the satellite images during the fight. The area was covered with an invisible shield of rays that did not allow any rays to penetrate it.

The old man was mad with happiness and decided to enjoy the victory with his close associates. In his excitement, he forgot to confirm the news to his Chinese counterparts.

Ashwathama entered the same saucer-like flying object alone wearing a life jacket wielding weapons unknown to mankind. Before entering it, he blessed everyone and told them not to expect him to return. His plan, he said, was to never return to this material world.

"*Jai Ashawthama,*" chanted all the people standing in the area with passion and respect.

The mercenaries were also told to get inside the aircraft. They meekly settled into a corner far away from the gigantic man. Once everyone was settled in, the saucer took off to the great Alps far away from the Himalayan mountain region.

Chapter 30
The End of an Era

The saucer reached its destination within a couple of hours and hovered in the sky for a bit before landing. The people inside the lab saw the saucer descending into a plain area. Sensing danger, the old man and the guard instructed the security forces to be on high alert. Ashwathama started pushing out the mercenaries one by one. The guards pointed their guns at the opening of the saucer, but to their dismay, all they saw was a heavy figure jumping out of the saucer roaring like a beast.

The guards started firing, but the heavy man retaliated with a bow and arrow type of weapon, which also looked very heavy. The arrows began to fly out of the bow at a frightening pace. The tip of each arrow had explosives that exploded as soon as it made contact.

The huge figure was wearing a heavy jacket that resisted all bullet strikes. He looked invincible and launched attacks at lightning speed.

The mercenaries tried to run away, but the arrows found their marks before they could move. Within minutes, all the guards standing in the plane area were killed.

The other guards coming out of the lab to strike were killed before they could even understand what was going on. Three helicopters suddenly came out of nowhere to fire at the figure, but were unable to because the explosive-tipped arrows came directly at them and exploded like missiles.

The fight continued and all the guards were killed one by one. Ashwathama began to destroy the lab with the arrows that he had once used during the great Kurukshetra battle. Soon, all the buildings were destroyed. The old man tried to run away, but he was no match for Ashwathama, who caught him and tied him up with ropes.

Ashwathama was in a destructive mood and killed whoever came before him with his deadly arrows. The whole area was destroyed within a couple of hours.

The old man lay at the feet of Ashwathama, who was resting after the long fight. Ashwathama knew about the importance of the old man from one of the nine unknown men who showed him the photo he had taken secretly when he had visited the place to retrieve the shell.

Ashwathama untied the old man and handed over some of the things he was carrying. The old man had no other option, but to start walking with Ashwathama towards the volcano.

Ashwathama had identified the location of the volcano using a sense that was lost to mankind over time. The journey was long and the old man got tired without any food or water. Realizing that the old man was falling behind, he scooped him up onto his shoulder on one side and put his belongings in the other hand. Being heavily built did not deter him – in fact, he did not look tired even after walking so many miles.

He gave the old man some of the food he was carrying and gave him the water he had collected from Himalayas before embarking on the journey. The journey continued for weeks along the forest terrains in the Alps, where they encountered various animal species.

When at last they reached their destination, Ashwathama got into a jovial mood. The volcano was visible in the distance and Ashwathama told the old man to bend over. Lifting his sword, he chanted something, looked up and with one blow, killed the old man.

Ashwathama then continued his journey and reached the mouth of the crater. He sat there for hours offering prayers to his favourite god Lord Shiva.

He finally jumped into the crater of the volcano as instructed by the god in his dreams.

Chapter 31

The Final Happening

After the final mission, the chief returned to his native place Hyderabad. The last couple of years felt like a fairytale in which he had a major role to play. But he had made a pact with the nine unknown men that he would not reveal their secrets to the outside world. He had promised to keep everything within himself for rest of the life.

Prabudh Upadhyay continued his services with NIA and has been part of many investigations concerned with national security. He was still taking guidance from Raju in many investigations.

The shell and the keys were stored in an untraceable location specially designed by the nine unknown men in an unknown place surrounded by Naga sadhus.

The nine unknown men continued with their experiments that benefitted mankind and planned to implement the results of some of their experiments to change the course of mankind.

Dr. Hiroshi went on to become one of the greatest disciples of the nine unknown men and started working with them on many experiments.

Narendra joined one of the political parties in India and became a great leader in due course of time. He began to implement the experimental results of the nine unknown men to change the future of the young generation in India.

The *suryavanshis* planned to build a new temple with the idol they got from the nine unknown men. The people in the village of warriors were so happy that they got a chance to serve their masters. All of them missed Ashwathama and planned to build a temple in his name.

Meanwhile in China, a high level plan was underway to retrieve the shell and the key…

To be continued……..

www.ingramcontent.com/pod-product-compliance
Lightning Source LLC
La Vergne TN
LVHW010018200726
843495LV00015B/1822